MASKED

An Israeli play
about three Palestinian brothers.

by Ilan Hatsor

Translated by Michael Taub

A SAMUEL FRENCH ACTING EDITION

New York Hollywood London Toronto

SAMUELFRENCH.COM

No one shall commit or authorize any act or omission by which the copy-right of, or the right to copyright, this play may be impaired.

No one shall make any changes in this play for the purpose of production.

Publication of this play does not imply availability for performance. Both amateurs and professionals considering a production are strongly advised in their own interests to apply to Samuel French, Inc., for written permission before starting rehearsals, advertising, or booking a theatre.

No part of this book may be reproduced, stored in a retrieval system, or transmitted in any form, by any means, now known or yet to be invented, including mechanical, electronic, photocopying, recording, videotaping, or otherwise, without the prior written permission of the publisher.

IMPORTANT BILLING AND CREDIT
REQUIREMENTS

All producers of MASKED *must* give credit to the Author of the Play in all programs distributed in connection with performances of the Play, and in all instances in which the title of the Play appears for the purposes of adver-tising, publicizing or otherwise exploiting the Play and /or a production. The name of the Author *must* appear on a separate line on which no other name appears, immediately following the title and *must* appear in size of type not less than fifty percent of the size of the title type.

MAYA PRODUCTIONS
THE SPLINTER GROUP
HIGHBROW ENTERTAINMENT

PRESENT

MASKED

by ILAN HATSOR

translation by MICHAEL TAUB

WITH

SANJIT DE SILVA   DAOUD HEIDAMI   ARIAN MOAYED

Scenic Design WILSON CHIN & OLA MASLIK	Costume Design JENNIFER CAPRIO
Lighting Design THOM WEAVER	Sound Design JOACHIM HORSELY
Music OMRI HASON	Fight Director CHRISTIAN KELLY-SORDELET
Press Representative KEITH SHERMAN AND ASSOCIATES	Advertising HOFSTETTER + PARTNERS AGENCY212
Marketing LEANNE SCHANZER PROMOTIONS INC.	Casting STUART HOWARD AMY SCHECTER/PAUL HARD
General Management THE SPLINTER GROUP	Management Associate CARLY DIFULVIO
Associate Producers STEVE KLEIN JANET PAILET/SHARON CARR	Production Stage Manager JANA LLYNN

Assistant Director
LISA BRAILOFF

directed by AMI DAYAN

AUTHOR'S NOTE

I wrote *Masked* in 1990 during the first year of my theatre studies in the Tel Aviv University. The first Intifada had broken out three years earlier and this extreme phenomena, which shattered the lives of Palestinians and Israelis, received no expression on the Israeli stage. I felt that close to our homes great dramas were taking place involving life and death dilemmas and decisions, and I needed to write about it.

I chose to tell this story from the point of view of three Palestinian brothers, utilizing the power of theatre to introduce the Israeli audience to it's enemy. It was a perspective different to the one they were accustomed; Palestinians not as faceless monsters, but as human beings forced to deal with unbearable dilemmas and conflicts.

During the writing process I never thought of my characters as 'Arabs' or 'Palestinians'. For me they were, and still are, three brothers. In this case they are Palestinians. They could just as easily have been Irish, Bosnians or Germans, victimized and manipulated by stronger and greater forces. The situations exposed in the play go beyond any particular nationalistic conflict and could have occurred (as indeed they have) in other times and places where occupation, oppression, civil war and the like have reigned.

Despite the political nature of the play I do not think it is the playwright's role to deliver a political message or a one-sided ideology to his audience as this will degrade the artistic endeavor, making it shallow and flat. In my view a playwright is to write a good drama, where each side's argument receives equal weight, raising questions that never have simple answers, with varied contradicting messages. As far as I am concerned, political theatre does not need to deal with ideas and ideologies, but with the human beings that are confronted by them.

Ilan Hatsor
New York City, 2007

CHARACTERS

KHALID, 18, the youngest brother, a new member in the leadership of the resistance.

NA'IM, Mid 20s, the middle brother, a senior member in the leadership of the resistance.

DAOUD, 30, the oldest brother, married, father of a baby, works in Israel.

TIME

Fall 1990, evening to dawn.

PLACE

A large Arab village in the West Bank. The action takes place in the back of a butcher shop. There are no windows. One door leads to the room, upstage right. The central area of the back wall is covered with blood stains. A big butcher block stands there. Hooks, butcher knives, and other instruments for handling meat are dirty from the day's business. Boxes, feathers, disorder.

SCENE 1

(Lights. **KHALID** *and* **NA'IM.** *)*

KHALID. What will they do to him?

NA'IM. They'll ask him a few questions.

KHALID. If it turns out he...

NA'IM. If it turns out.

KHALID. Talk to them, Na'im.

NA'IM. I did. They gave him a break. A gift. Thanks to me, I want you to know.

KHALID. It's a mistake, Na'im. Our own brother...

NA'IM. Stop it. You tell me. A week ago, was he here on the day of the arrests?

KHALID. How? He works. In Tel Aviv. We've got to do something. You go talk to them, and I'll go to Daoud.

NA'IM. I'm not talking to anyone anymore. Let Daoud speak for himself, and I hope he's got something to say. And you, you stay right here and don't do anything except what I tell you, understand?

KHALID. But Daoud has to know.

NA'IM. I'll tell him.

KHALID. It's a scam. The whole story. Abu Raduan, a born thief, is badmouthing Daoud, your brother. We caught him stealing sheep from father once, you and me, remember? –

NA'IM. *(Interrupting* **KHALID***)* Abu Raduan stabbed that Israeli officer with his own hands. Not to mention all the other things he's done.

KHALID. Yeah. So now he's the village hero. Still, I don't believe a word he says. The Intifada didn't make him an honest man.

NA'IM. Everything from before the Intifada is dead. Today everyone has to prove himself. Abu Raduan did, and people believe him...the problem is, he says he saw Daoud in the Secret Service car — the Shabak!

KHALID. He's lying!

NA'IM. There were others with him.

KHALID. Did you talk to them?

NA'IM. Not yet.

KHALID. You see?

NA'IM. They'll be here tonight.

(Short pause.)

KHALID. Maybe he got arrested.

NA'IM. Then why didn't he say anything? A thing like that you talk about, don't you? Tell me, was he here at all during the day of the arrests?

KHALID. I told you, he was working in Tel Aviv.

NA'IM. And he spent the night there too?

KHALID. Yes, he stays sometimes. Lucky for the both of you that you weren't in the village that night. They shot anyone who tried to run. They were all over the hills. They turned the night into day with their flares. There must have been a thousand soldiers — and helicopters, four of them, up there. They went crazy.

NA'IM. Did they get to our house?

KHALID. No. They didn't even bother. They knew exactly where to go. They searched and found.

NA'IM. And Ataf? How did he die?

KHALID. They knocked on his door, he jumped out the window...they shot him...he died...on the spot. (Silence. KHALID comes near NA'IM) How are you, Na'im? How is life in the mountains? I've missed you.

NA'IM. I'm ok. I missed you too. You, mother, Daoud too. In the mountains? It's not easy. I'm not alone, though. There are people there with me. Everybody's on the run. Someday, you'll meet them. They're doing things, not like the shitheads in the village. (NA'IM stands and moves away from KHALID) Why didn't he come back?!

KHALID. He was working. He works. Somebody's got to make money now.

NA'IM. He needs lots of money now...

KHALID. He feeds us all. And his wife is pregnant again.

NA'IM. Does he talk about me?

KHALID. Yes. He's upset. Like father. But I know he's worried about you.

NA'IM. And mother?

KHALID. She cries for you all the time.

NA'IM. Our own brother, Daoud...Go get him!

KHALID. Just think a minute, Na'im. He's got a young wife and a baby. He's building a house now, he's not going to risk it all. Daoud is a rational man.

NA'IM. Too rational. That's what upsets me. Go get him.

KHALID. But he knows what's happening. He's not going to throw everything away for someone, or some idea. If anything happens to him...could you look father and mother in the eye?

NA'IM. Can I look at them today?

KHALID. And his wife and baby? How will the baby grow up?

NA'IM. Anyone who betrays his people betrays his wife and children too. If it's true.

KHALID. Let's see you tell that to his wife. Or to our parents. No. You won't tell them. You'll run to the mountains and leave me to deal with the mess, the way you did at the rally.

NA'IM. The rally.!... maybe he knew...thought about it? The same day Nidal...

KHALID. Nidal?! I think we should both shut up...especially you.

NA'IM. Then shut up and bring him here, now. We've got to talk about that too.

KHALID. No.

NA'IM. If Daoud knew...before the rally...that the army was coming...

KHALID. He came and begged us not to take Nidal, but you sent him away. You didn't listen.

NA'IM. That's what I'm trying to tell you.

KHALID. You didn't want to listen.

NA'IM. Those who knew and warned us, also made sure the army would be there.

KHALID. You didn't listen. We shouldn't have taken Nidal. Because of us...!... we...you said you'd watch him...you promised, and I believed you.

NA'IM. Enough! Nobody thought anything would happen to Nidal. Daoud was always a coward. How could I know? How could I know? Khalid, we didn't shoot Nidal. *(Pause)* Go get him!

KHALID. What will they do to him?

NA'IM. I won't let them touch him, but without me he doesn't stand a chance. You've got to bring him here today and that's that. It's up to the leadership now.

KHALID. You're crazy. Who'll believe him?

NA'IM. I will. But he's got to come now, before the leadership arrives. I want to hear him. If he's clean, nobody will touch him. They'll have to deal with me. And nobody should hear about this.

KHALID. Will you help him?

NA'IM. Yes, but you have to help me. He's my brother too, isn't he? We haven't talked since then...since the rally... maybe the tragedy did something to him...make up your mind. We only have an hour.

KHALID. I can't. I can't. I'm scared. Like when I took Nidal home...I never told you about it. After you ran away...the Israelis... they went nuts...bullets...tear gas. People were falling...screaming. I was running around in the middle of the craziness, without feeling, in a daze, like a robot. The only thing on my mind was to find the boy. To find the boy. Suddenly I saw a group of women. They were standing there screaming like black crows. And I could tell. I ran...pushed...they let me through, whispering "It's his brother. It's his brother." And I saw him. He was lying there, like a little angel. An angel with a red hole in his forehead. I picked him up. He was warm. His eyes...I started walking. Everyone, even the soldiers in the street, looked away. I walked and kissed him... walked and kissed him...I could smell him...his hair... At home, mother and father stood at the gate. Mother screamed and started pulling her hair, and father...he grabbed the boy out of my arms, carried him into the house and slammed the door in my face. Poor Nidal, our baby brother…if only he had died...but he just lies there all day...drooling and wetting his pants...*(Pause)* I'll have no part of that. I'm going to talk with Daoud.

NA'IM. Khalid!

KHALID. I'm going.

NA'IM. You're not going anywhere. You're breaking a strict order of the leadership.

KHALID. So are you. Aren't you? They said only in an hour.

NA'IM. Khalid!

KHALID. Daoud is more important.

(**KHALID** *tries to leave, but* **NA'IM** *grabs him*)

NA'IM. Don't go. Wait!

KHALID. And if I don't, then what?

NA'IM. Stop it! I'm just trying to stop this. Don't you understand? Don't you understand anything? You think I've made it all up? Some other people in this village are being dealt with already. Right now. Daoud is the only one they gave a break. Tonight at eight. The whole leadership will be here, but he better be prepared. You're right. I'm not allowed to talk with him before that, but I have to know. There's no other way. It's not something I made up.

KHALID. He must run away!

NA'IM. Listen to me a sec, Khalid. Daoud's a marked man! His life isn't worth anything anymore. The traitor who thought he'd be able to hide here after he ran away from Ramallah — we knew about him before he even arrived. If Daoud tries to run, they'll know where to go.

You want trouble? The leadership is planning a raid on the village tonight.

KHALID. Raid? What raid? What happened?

NA'IM. What happened? You live here and see nothing? The arrests, last week. The Israelis came down on us hard. Everything's ruined. The old timers are in jail. We have to start from scratch. We must take care of those whose homes they blew up. Nobody's looking out for them, and they're falling apart. We need some instructions from headquarters...that's why we came here today...

KHALID. But we're talking about Daoud...

NA'IM. That's the main point! Nothing we do here means anything so long as the squealers are loose in the village. How would the Israelis succeed without these rats? Is there any other way? This village is going to be cleaned up tonight.

KHALID. Terrific! You learned something from the Israeli's...

NA'IM. This is war, habibi. If you're going to warn him, you'll just get him in more trouble. There's no other way, but the truth. Either he is or he's not.

KHALID. What do you think?

NA'IM. He's clean. There's no other way. If you believe it too, go get him.

KHALID. OK. I'll bring him here. Just promise me!—

NA'IM. Alright. Now listen, don't you dare sniff around his house. Send some kid to call him. Make sure he doesn't suspect anything. Think up some story. Think of something. *(Impatient)* It's dark already. I have to go.

KHALID. Where are you going? I don't want to be here alone with him, Na'im.

NA'IM. It's late. I've got to be at Issam's.

KHALID. Issam's?

NA'IM. A little business. Not for long. Nothing to do with Daoud. I hope. Keep him here without telling him anything. I'm gone. (NA'IM *exits.*)

KHALID. There's nothing to say.

NA'IM. *(Re-entering—)* With all this craziness I almost forgot. Lots of people are talking about you. Good things. I hear it all the time. Tomorrow, hopefully, things will work out. Maybe you'll get a position...

KHALID. Me?

NA'IM. That's right, but don't ask, because I'm not telling.

KHALID. What position?

NA'IM. Prime Minister of Palestine.

(NA'IM *exits. Lights fade to black.*)

SCENE 2

(Half an hour later. Lights up on KHALID *cleaning the blood-stained back wall. After a while* DAOUD *enters carrying a large jar of olives. At first he does not see* KHALID.*)*

DAOUD. "Ahalan." *(He spots* KHALID.*)* Hey, Khalid. *(They hug.)* What's going on?

KHALID. You came quick. *(*KHALID *resumes his cleaning.)*

DAOUD. I just got home from work, Shukri's kid came by, he said you needed some help, so I came right away.

KHALID. What's with the olives?

DAOUD. I stopped at Shukri's. I saw him and remembered his father, Abu Shukri may he rest in peace. Two ugly men…. Did you know. once Shukri got an olive in his ear. And it got stuck there. He went for a week with that olive in his ear till it dried up and fell out. Lucky the olive didn't grow in his ear. My boss Moshe's been driving me crazy for two weeks to bring him some olives. He's crazy about our olives. So I went to buy some from Shukri's wife. God, is she ugly!

KHALID. And you're Mr. Handsome.

DAOUD. You never knew Abu Shukri, huh? The father was even uglier then the son! Shukri's a beauty queen next to him. Whenever Na'im and I wouldn't eat, mother would threaten us that Abu Shukri will come take us at night if we didn't finish our plates. They're ugly, but they sure know how to prepare olives.

KHALID. How's the baby?

DAOUD. Coughing. Amal says it's from the tear gas, from last week's roundups. Why did they use gas? These Israelis… to hell with them…there wasn't even real rioting. She'll take him to the doctor in Nablus tomorrow. I'd go with her, but my job…

KHALID. I'll take her. I also breathed some gas.

DAOUD. You? For you it's like perfume. *(They laugh.)* Thanks.

KHALID. Maybe you shouldn't have come?

DAOUD. What are brothers for? Where's the owner?

KHALID. In the administration building. Did you know they picked up his son last week? He was there every day since. But they won't even tell him where the kid is locked up.

DAOUD. Lucky they didn't blow up his home. That son of his brought him only trouble.

KHALID. I don't know. I help when it's needed, and don't ask questions. Today here. Yesterday Kassam's wife. Whatever.

DAOUD. I'd help Kassam's wife myself...

KHALID. I helped her with the seeds.

DAOUD. I'd help her with some seeds too.

KHALID. Stop it. They helped us too...with Nidal.

DAOUD. And they stopped after a week. *(After a brief pause, impatiently.)* Ok, you wanted help... where are the sacks? Should we go?

KHALID. Let me finish. Father said you wanted to talk with me.

DAOUD. We'll talk at home. How many sacks are there to carry?

KHALID. Two.

DAOUD. You call me for that? At your age I used to carry two sacks on my back, one in each hand, and another on my —

KHALID. We heard about you —

DAOUD. You're cleaning up this dump like it was the White House. I'm tired, hungry, filthy, horny —"Ya'lla"— let's go.

KHALID. Five more minutes. How's the car?

DAOUD. It runs. The problem is, getting through. They searched. One hour on the road, four at the road-blocks. I.D. I.D., I.D. ID. — Four times I showed it.

*(**KHALID** gestures for **DAOUD** to hold the rag he is using for a moment, as he lifts something. **DAOUD** does so reluctantly, then.)*

Tell me "Ayooni," precious, don't I deserve a piece of meat for the work I put in around here...?

*(The door opens, **NA'IM** rushes in. He rushes to the down-stage corner of the room and rinses his hands. **DAOUD** is taken aback for a second, then realizes it's **NA'IM**.)*

DAOUD. Na'im...?

NA'IM. Daoud! Khalid...Khalid!

*(**NA'IM** embraces **KHALID**.)*

DAOUD. I didn't think...such a long time...

NA'IM. Yeah.

*(**KHALID** resumes his washing off the blood from the back wall, cleaning knives etc.)*

DAOUD. I dreamt about you...I swear...last night.

NA'IM. Really? What about?

DAOUD. That we met...and here you are...it's about time.

NA'IM. Yes, it's about time.

DAOUD. Sure. *(Ill-at-ease)* It's good to see you. Where have you been?

NA'IM. In the mountains.

DAOUD. What do you eat?

NA'IM. Whatever there is.

DAOUD. *(To **KHALID**.)* What answers...How long are you staying for?

NA'IM. A few hours.

DAOUD. Still, you do need a few hours at home.

NA'IM. You deserve congratulations. A baby boy, heh?

DAOUD. Yes. *(They shake hands mid stage.)* A son. So small. And again, Amal's preg—

NA'IM. *(Moves away.)* That's great. It's important. What's his name?

DAOUD. When he was born...there was only one name we could give him...*(Pause.)* Nidal. You have to see him. Mother says he looks like you.

NA'IM. *(Laughs.)* She says that about every baby.

DAOUD. Why are we here? Come to my place.

NA'IM. No, this is fine.

DAOUD. Come on! Take a shower. Have a hot meal. We'll talk...then you'll go.

NA'IM. I can't even go into my own home, so how can I—

DAOUD. You don't want to go there. They're watching the place...

KHALID. What are you talking about?

DAOUD. *(To* **NA'IM***)* You know, Khalid sees everything better than the rest of us. Only he doesn't know how to piece things together yet. What do you think of him, this kid brother of ours?

NA'IM. I say he's a man!

DAOUD. Ah...I liked him even better as a kid. **(DAOUD** *pokes at* **KHALID** *in play.)* Well, what are we waiting for, let's go to my place.

NA'IM. You're forgetting my situation.

DAOUD. It's dark outside. Come on.

NA'IM. The squealers haven't gone to bed yet. We're staying here. **(NA'IM** *sits.)*

DAOUD. You're so stubborn. Tell us, Na'im, according to stories I hear. you're already a hero.

NA'IM. Don't believe it...believe your olives.

DAOUD. When can you come back?

NA'IM. I don't know. It's dangerous. How are things with you, Daoud? You look...

DAOUD. Tired? I just got back from work.

NA'IM. Still in Tel Aviv? At that restaurant?

DAOUD. Where you saw me.

NA'IM. Today Tel Aviv is like...another planet.

DAOUD. Be grateful. Believe me, it's better to live like a mountain-goat than work for them every day.

NA'IM. Really?

DAOUD. These Israelis, they get under your skin, and they won't come out...can't get rid of them.

NA'IM. *(Surprised.)* Oh...

DAOUD. Nowhere. Going to work, at work, coming back home... You get home and want to rest — bang! Detentions. What do they think? That Arafat is hiding in the village? These Israelis. Here, look at this. *(Pulls out and hands* NA'IM *a piece of paper.)*

NA'IM. What is it?

DAOUD. A summons. To the courthouse, in Nablus. For me.

NA'IM. Congratulations, Daoud! Are you a suspect?

DAOUD. Me? God, no. It's a hearing for that officer who shot Nidal. Want to come?

NA'IM. You're joking.

DAOUD. No. They're joking. With their officers and their fat lawyers...me, I'm crying! They make everything sound so proper. By the book. Shooting only below the knees...

NA'IM. Their knees are about the height of a kid's head. Don't forget that.

DAOUD. Then why the whole show?

NA'IM. They do it for themselves. Problems with their conscience. It's a waste of time, Daoud. Their law is about justice their way, not ours. *(*NA'IM *tosses the summons to the floor.* DAOUD *picks it up, and places it back in his pocket.)*

DAOUD. I bet you have your own way with justice now.

NA'IM. Of course...but there are more important things to do. How about you?

DAOUD. Same old thing.

NA'IM. But you...you work for them...

DAOUD. So what? What do you want?! You want us to starve? You bend a little, wait for the dust to settle. We had it...tired of it...we've had it. *(Pause.)* I want to tell you something.

NA'IM. I'm listening.

DAOUD. Today...after all we've been through...with Nidal, and you having to run away...this is still your home...

you understand? Sometimes I lie in bed, it's cold and raining, and I think about you...wonder if you need anything...tell me...clothes, food, money. Do you need any money? Don't be shy. We're brothers.

NA'IM. I hope so.

DAOUD. You can come visit me. Not just Khalid.

NA'IM. He said you were mad at me.

(*Pause.*)

DAOUD. (*Gives* KHALID *a sharp look.*) True...there was a time... when I was mad. But I'm not like father. For him you're dead. He's a rock. Me...I've forgiven.

NA'IM. Forgiven what, Daoud?

DAOUD. Drop it, Na'im.

NA'IM. Why? We don't meet every day. So let's talk.

DAOUD. Where will it get you?

NA'IM. I don't know. Anything is better than what we have now.

KHALID. (*Interrupts.*) That's not true, Na'im.

NA'IM. Khalid! Keep out of this, habibi. What do you mean, you've forgiven me? Forgiven me for what? What are you being so nice about? Spit it out, Daoud. Everything, everything you got on me. Maybe you'll hear a few things from me too.

DAOUD. I heard you then… Last time we met. Before the rally. You had all the answers. But you were mistaken. What a mistake...

NA'IM. Yes. A mistake. A big one. You know which one?

DAOUD. Yes. Taking Nidal, though I warned you the army was coming.

NA'IM. That was no mistake. An older brother showing his brother a rally by free Palestinians. Nowadays that's the proper thing to do. My mistake that day was, I never stopped asking myself and you a question I could never answer...How did you know the army was coming?

DAOUD. A seven-year old child...a seven-year old...You gave him a flag, you put him in a uniform....and you took him...and turned him into a martyr. A "Shahid". A seven-year old "Shahid"! My God! What have we come to?

NA'IM. How did you know?

DAOUD. And you still have questions? What did you come here for? What next should we expect from you, Na'im? What? And you, Khalid, why did you bring me here?

NA'IM. Maybe you didn't hear me. How did you know the army was coming?

DAOUD. (*To* KHALID.) What was that story of yours, with the cement bags?

KHALID. I wanted you to meet.

DAOUD. For this? It's a waste of time. *(to* NA'IM*)* You were crazy before you ran away, but now...what are they doing to you, Na'im? What kind of poison are they feeding you...

NA'IM. You're still not answering.

DAOUD. What kind of monsters are you hanging out with? Look at your clothes. What's that? Blood...

NA'IM. Blood! You know what? I'm a murderer. And a madman. And the family trouble-maker. Anything else? But none of that answers how you knew the army was coming.

DAOUD. God, you're stubborn. It's so simple. I saw them on my way home from work. That's all.

NA'IM. We'd posted twenty guards, as early as noon, and no one saw a thing.

DAOUD. Shows you what they're worth, eh?

NA'IM. Why did you stay in Tel Aviv last week?

DAOUD. During the arrests? (NA'IM *nods.)* You asshole. You really are an asshole. I had to work. The Israelis had a holiday. There was lots of work. I slept there. Now, did that answer your question? I spent one night in Tel Aviv. Anything wrong with that? It happened to work out for the best, in fact.

NA'IM. Happened to? Some people see it differently.

DAOUD. So, you are here to warn me... Really, thanks a lot.

Don't worry about me. You can tell them that...*(DAOUD begins to leave.)*

NA'IM. You tell them!

DAOUD. What...whom...what do you want from my life?

NA'IM. Nothing...nothing...

DAOUD. Khalid, what's going on here?

NA'IM. Leave him alone. Talk to me.

DAOUD. It's impossible. You haven't changed!

NA'IM. And you?! Have you?

KHALID. Stop it, both of you! Listen, Daoud. Just listen. This isn't a game. This is life or death!

DAOUD. Whose?

NA'IM. Yours!

DAOUD. *(Shocked.)* What...what are you talking about?

NA'IM. They think you're a collaborator.

DAOUD. Who thinks that?

KHALID. The leadership, today...

NA'IM. *(Stops him.)* Not a word about the leadership.

DAOUD. *(Worked up.)* You too? Him too?

KHALID. Yes! ...No. What difference does it make? What counts is...

DAOUD. You've met already! You already talked!

KHALID. Yes.

DAOUD. He's messing with your brains again! *(To NA'IM)* Run away...for months I've been swallowing the shit you left behind when you ran away. Now you come here...a guest...and allow yourself to talk as if I...One day...one day you'll do what I do every day, make a living for this family. One day you'll take care of poor Nidal the way Khalid does every day. No. Not you. You have to be a big shot...a rebel...a fighter...sh...sh...Underground...moving from place to place...But at whose expense? Whose? Mother's? Father's? And now mine, and Khalid's? And Nidal's? At Nidal's expense...Come home and take a good look at him once. At this vegetable who could be living today if you and your—.

NA'IM. *(Yells.)* If this village could get rid of the dogs who led the army to our rally. Careful Daoud. Your whole story... God only knows what I'm going through. Them...and you...and me in the middle.

DAOUD. You're not in the middle. You're with them. And I'm not against you. I hope you make it. But leave me out of it. I'm going. I've got things to do. And if this is why you came here, it's better you never come back again.

(DAOUD begins to leave, but NA'IM grabs him.)

NA'IM. Are you getting anything I'm saying? You'd better listen very carefully to what I'm saying. And just remember one thing. if it wasn't for your brother you'd be dead now.

DAOUD. What?

NA'IM. You're a marked man.

DAOUD. Why? What are you talking about?

NA'IM. The leadership. They're supposed to be here today. Soon. They're angry, you know. They've got some tough questions. They want answers...Do yourself a favor, start cooperating. I want to help you.

DAOUD. Sure...*(Pause.)* I'm going. I've had enough.

NA'IM. There's nowhere for you to go. They're all over the village. Thanks to me you'll get a chance to defend yourself. That's much more than the others got...but you must be ready...and me too.

DAOUD. What...what have I done?

NA'IM. You'll find out. From this moment on, you have no more questions. Just me. You just do the answering.

(NA'IM turns a waste-bin over, turning it into a stool, and positions it center stage. He points DAOUD to it. DAOUD hesitates, then sits. Immediately NA'IM slaps DAOUD hard.)

That's just a "hello" from the leadership. And there's more. Do you know what happens to collaborators? Do you know how they die? You do know. I've seen it.

You're my brother, and I want to help you get through it. But even if I do believe you I've got to ask you the questions they'll be asking. Together we'll pull through this. Ok? Be strong. And remember! They don't know about Nidal. Some day we'll settle that between us. Should we begin? *(Pause.)* When was the last time you met with Israeli agents?

DAOUD. Never.

NA'IM. When was the last time you met with Israeli agents?

DAOUD. I don't know any Israeli agents.

NA'IM. The problem is you were seen with them a week before the arrests.

DAOUD. Where? When?

NA'IM. You tell me that.

DAOUD. Never. Nowhere.

NA'IM. And I'm telling you it was in Nablus two weeks ago.

DAOUD. In Nablus...what would I be doing in Nablus?

KHALID. *(Gently.)* Try to remember, Daoud.

DAOUD. Oh yeah. I was buying a crib.

NA'IM. Congrats. After shopping, what did you do?

DAOUD. When?

NA'IM. At noon.

DAOUD. I came back here.

NA'IM. How?

DAOUD. On a camel. What do you mean "how"? By bus.

NA'IM. And what did you do before that?

DAOUD. *(Amused.)* I read the paper, ate some peanuts...

NA'IM. This isn't funny. You were seen riding with Israeli Secret Service agents.

DAOUD. It's a lie! Who saw me?

NA'IM. Never mind that...

KHALID. Tell him...

NA'IM. Never mind I said! Don't interfere!

DAOUD. It's actually very important. Nowadays, to get rid of someone, all you have to do is spread some dirt, make people believe it...

KHALID. What are you going on about?

DAOUD. Listen to the kid. What do you know about the people they kill?

KHALID. That they're stinking traitors.

DAOUD. That's what your leadership feeds you. Sometimes it's true, but not always. Want an example? How about Munir? Why did he die?

KHALID. He was pushing stuff.

DAOUD. Bullshit! He was a farmer and he would have stayed one if you *(To* **NA'IM***)* hadn't killed him. *(To* **KHALID***)* Someone planted the stuff on him. Someone who had a bone to pick with him over a piece of land. *(To* **NA'IM***)* Am I lying? Believe me Na'im, everyone smells. Your heroes too.

NA'IM. Munir is dead. He won't help you now.

DAOUD. No he can't. But it would help to know who set me up. Tell me the name, and I'll tell you the reason

NA'IM. The person who saw you...was not alone. There were others with him.

DAOUD. ...And I'm not supposed to know that either.

NA'IM. *(Angered)* Arafat's wife, mother and younger sister. You're just playing for time. Did you go with the Israelis or not?

DAOUD. They saw me?

NA'IM. Yes. They testified against you. *(Pause.* **DAOUD** *shakes his head slowly.)*

DAOUD. Alright...Alright... *(To* **KHALID***)* I didn't want you to know this... *(To* **NA'IM***)* the next day I had to go back...to return the crib. I couldn't put it together. *(To* **KHALID***)* You tried too!

*(***NA'IM*** glances at* **KHALID** *who nods.)*

As soon as I get to the store — wham! Two fire bombs, they hit the Israeli patrol vehicle. The usual — curfew, searches, commotion. How is this connected with me? I wanted to go home. I took the side streets, almost got out of town, when suddenly this car pulls up. And me, still with the crib on my head.

NA'IM. The Secret Service car!

DAOUD. Yes. There was a curfew. You know, they were really nice. Papers, searches, the usual, but then they offered me a ride in their car. I told them I appreciate it, but it wasn't in my direction. They insisted. So did I, but eventually they talked me into it.

NA'IM. How?

DAOUD. With a fist in the face and a kick in the balls! They took me in, *(Pause.)* arrested me. Got that?

NA'IM. We got it.

DAOUD. *(To **KHALID**)* I didn't want to worry you.

NA'IM. Keep talking!

DAOUD. They took me to their headquarters. Then this officer shows up, the chief in charge of the village. He wanted names of leaders— I told him I didn't know any.

NA'IM. How come a week later they knew exactly who is who?

DAOUD. Aren't there enough informers in the village?

NA'IM. Yes there are.

DAOUD. I didn't tell them anything, because I don't know anything, and I don't want to either. You know how much I'm interested in you guys...

NA'IM. And that's all? They just let you go?

DAOUD. Sure. They could tell I wasn't involved.

NA'IM. I wonder how you convinced them.

DAOUD. Look at me Na'im! Do I look like a rebel to you?! With a crib over my head?

NA'IM. Do they know anything about me?

DAOUD. Do I work with them? How should I know?

NA'IM. So you left.

DAOUD. Yes. *(Pause.)* I'm telling you. I simply explained to them...

NA'IM. "Explained to them." If they worked you over, the Israeli agents, you wouldn't stand on your feet for a week. Certainly not be able to walk. Or, maybe it was a pleasant talk?...you're in this deep, Daoud.

DAOUD. That's what you think!

NA'IM. That's what they think, and they know a thing or two about Israeli agents.

DAOUD. But they don't know me. Right? You do! You know I would never do such a thing. Especially not after Nidal...

NA'IM. Hold it right there, Daoud. I've already told you nobody knows you warned me about the army coming to the rally, and that's how it stands. That would only complicate things for you.

DAOUD. And for you too! You were supposed to report to them, weren't you? How you abandoned that child in the middle of hell. Would you abandon them too? *(To* **KHALID***)* Maybe we shouldn't trust him so much. Maybe our hero is nothing but a little coward.

NA'IM. I didn't run away. I don't run away from anything. Nidal just panicked and let go of my hand. I couldn't go looking for him. I was in uniform and the soldiers were shooting like crazy. It would have been more dangerous for him! I hid and waited. I couldn't come out before nightfall.

DAOUD. But Nidal was with you. You were responsible for him.

NA'IM. True, and to this day I can't forgive myself. I never will, but there's someone who told the army about our rally. And me...I can't manage everything myself. I want you to swear that you don't know, that you never heard who brought the soldiers who shot Nidal.

DAOUD. I could strangle him with my bare hands. But what am I? What am I? People don't discuss things like this with me. Why these questions, Na'im?

NA'IM. Did you tell anyone?

DAOUD. What?

NA'IM. That you were stopped, in Nablus?

DAOUD. My wife...Amal—

NA'IM. No good. They won't believe her. A friend? Someone believable?

DAOUD. No. Why?

NA'IM. I'd bring them to testify for you.

KHALID. Why didn't you tell me?

DAOUD. Do the two of you tell me everything you do? I didn't want you to know. And then, a week later, after they rounded up the leadership, I was already scared. I knew someone would get ideas...as if I...

KHALID. You should have said something. To me, at least.

DAOUD. Yes. I made a mistake.

KHALID. I wouldn't have told anyone.

NA'IM. That was the first time you met with them?

DAOUD. The first, and hopefully, the last. *(Pause.)*

NA'IM. I hope they buy it.

DAOUD. *(Rising)* OK, so is that it with this interrogation?

NA'IM. Sit! That is just a taste of the real interrogation.

DAOUD. *(Goes to leave, finds the door locked.)* Give me the key. *(Pause.)* Give me the key Khalid!

(KHALID looks for the key at it's hiding place. Not finding it, he looks angrily at NA'IM.)

Like this? You tie up the calf and they arrive for the slaughter? Me! Your brother! This is your justice? Someone anonymously frames you, and then good luck proving yourself? You forgot who I am!

NA'IM. No, Daoud. I just hope you didn't forget who you are!

(NA'IM gives DAOUD the key. DAOUD begins to leave cursing, KHALID tries to stop him—)

KHALID. Wait Daoud. What are you doing, Na'im? You can't leave. They're all over the village.

(DAOUD exits. KHALID runs after him, but NA'IM stops him. After a pause, DAOUD returns and quickly locks the door, clearly shocked by what he has encountered outside. Pause.)

KHALID. What should we do now?

NA'IM. We wait. He'll tell it all to the committee.

KHALID. And you?

> (**NA'IM** *is silent.*)

> …And what will happen?

> (**NA'IM** is silent.)

DAOUD. Khalid, this is all crazy. Make him tell me who squealed on me.

KHALID. Na'im…

NA'IM. I can't.

DAOUD. Ok. Then I'll just sit here and shut all of you up. When are they coming? In an hour? Fine. I have ways to defend myself.

NA'IM. Are you sure?

DAOUD. Yes. And I have some news for you too.

> (**DAOUD** *tosses the key back to* **NA'IM.**)

NA'IM. News?

DAOUD. There's one guy…

NA'IM. What about him?

DAOUD. An informer. A few years already.

NA'IM. It's alright. We know who they are.

DAOUD. I'm sure the guy knows who he is, but no one else, because he's planted, nice and deep among you.

NA'IM. Planted? Who?

DAOUD. Who smeared my name?

NA'IM. You'll find out.

DAOUD. Ok.

> (*Pause.*)

NA'IM. Who? It could help you.

DAOUD. What I know is worth a lot more to you.

KHALID. (*To* **NA'IM**) Tell him.

NA'IM. No.

KHALID. (*After a short, tense pause-*) It's Abu Raduan.

DAOUD. (*Shocked-*) What?

KHALID. That's who.

DAOUD. That's...that's impossible.

NA'IM. Why?

DAOUD. Abu Raduan? That fat snitch? *(Laughs.)* That stinking pig? Him, you believe?! *(Laughing.)* The world's gone mad! My own brothers believe the biggest double dealer in the whole village. Him! He's been informing on us for five years already. He's on their payroll. So help me God. Abu Raduan...he's the answer to your questions.

NA'IM. You forgot that Abu Raduan stabbed an Israeli officer with his own hands!

DAOUD. *(Laughing.)* That's a legend by now...the officer fell and hurt himself, and Abu Raduan caught a free ride... to impress you...bunch of idiots. Abu Raduan... A favorite of the Israeli agents. *(NA'IM smiles, goes to the corner of the room and washes his face.)* And there's something else, Na'im.

KHALID. What?

DAOUD. Abu Raduan...you'd kill him.

KHALID. Why?

DAOUD. Abu Raduan...if you knew...you'd shoot him right away.

KHALID. What's to know?

DAOUD. Abu Raduan doesn't only want to get your brother killed. He also killed your best friend. Ataf.

(Pause.)

KHALID. He killed him?

DAOUD. Yes. He waited for him outside his house, because he knew Ataf would be running away, and he shot him.

KHALID. Why?

DAOUD. Because Abu Raduan was afraid Ataf knew about him. *(Incredulous.)* Why...?!

KHALID. But the soldiers...

DAOUD. No. They did not shoot him. *(Pause.)* What do you say to that? Take a good look at your people, Na'im. Scum, that's what they are.

KHALID. You see, Na'im...

NA'IM. How did you know that? Only one person in the whole village suspected Abu Raduan. Ataf. And he told me. Only me. He also told me that Abu Raduan was scared of him. Ataf wouldn't tell it to a shit like you. So how did you know?

DAOUD. *(Stammers)* I'll... I'll explain, Na'im—

NA'IM. What will you explain? You were not in the village. You were in Tel Aviv, right? In a restaurant. Cleaning up Jewish shit. How could you have known? You and Abu Raduan...Two scorpions begin stinging each other, after stinging the whole village.

DAOUD. It isn't too late... listen—

NA'IM. What's not too late?! To bring Ataf back? To release everyone they detained. To rebuild the homes they blew up? To cure Nidal? What isn't it too late for? You scum!

DAOUD. I am clean.

NA'IM. Not if you knew about Ataf. *(Pause.)* And your home? ...What a nice home you built since I left. From what? From what?

DAOUD. I work.

NA'IM. But you're supporting two families, aren't you? From what?

DAOUD. They gave me a loan at work...

NA'IM. A loan to an Arab dishwasher? You bring olives for your boss, but did they cover your bus fare when you were stuck?...You sent for me to bring you money...How did you build your house?

KHALID. Tell him, Daoud.

DAOUD. That has nothing to do with it, Khalid!—

KHALID. He took bricks from houses the Israeli's destroyed.

(Brief pause.)

NA'IM. What?!! …Never mind, never mind. One needs more than bricks to build a house. Where did you get the money? Where?

DAOUD. My own two hands...

NA'IM. Stop lying to me! Your home stinks from the bottom up.

DAOUD. My own hands...

NA'IM. You scum. You know what they do to homes of people like you?

DAOUD. I'm clean...I took a loan...

NA'IM. You can't do anything anymore. Your home… It's gone.

DAOUD. What...it's my home...my home...nagh, I just came from there...everything's OK...it's my home…Let me out!

NA'IM. Too late. There's nothing you can do anymore.

DAOUD. Nothing? I can blow up the whole world. It's my home. Even the Israelis give you time before they blow up your home.

NA'IM. Go to them!

DAOUD. All my things...I'll burn you all.

NA'IM. You already have.

DAOUD. I'll go to the army...

NA'IM. You already went.

DAOUD. My home...and you...

NA'IM. Had you been there...they'd have burned you too!

DAOUD. Amal...and the baby.

NA'IM. They're safe.

DAOUD. Safe?! With you?

NA'IM. Yes. They're safe, even if...

DAOUD. And all this time, you were here talking to me, while your friends were burning down my house? You bastard! Where are they? What have you done to them?

NA'IM. I told you. They're safe. I'm worried about you.

DAOUD. *(Screaming.)* Let me out. Let me out!!

NA'IM. Daoud, the only way out is straight into their knives.

DAOUD. *(Pause.)* You never really wanted to help me.

NA'IM. I did, and still do. Except that it is becoming more difficult every minute. If you were anyone else...I... with my own two hands...people like you...now listen, you don't have a home, no car, no T.V., no friends, no nothing. So now let's have the truth. From the beginning. All of it. I'm the only one standing between you and them. I don't want any surprises with the leadership. Speak!

DAOUD. You think I'd risk my life for anything else...for you...and Khalid. For you, and for the kid...you got me into this. That's right. I gave them names. In Nablus two weeks ago...they said they would pick up Khalid. Arrest him...and you, they said they would kill. There were four or five interrogators working me over. They pressured me. They said they'd kill you. They showed me pictures of Khalid in demonstrations, throwing stones, burning tires, they said they'd give him a year's administrative detention. No trial, just like that. One of them said...they'd send Amal back to Jordan because her family is there...with the baby...that they'd destroy my home because I didn't have a permit...they knew everything about me—they drove me nuts...all of them talking together. They said they'd make me look like an informer, that they'd have me walk through the village with them as they arrest people...as if I was leading them, and then they'd leave me on my own in the middle of the village, to be lynched. I was in a daze. I threw them a few names...I don't even know if they're leaders...They can do anything...everything they threatened to do...Who can stop them? I wasn't worried about myself. It was you! And him. When you're the oldest brother, you've got to keep the family going. That is what an older brother is supposed to do. I let up once... And *(In tears.)* Nidal...*(Pause.)* ... me too...maybe I didn't explain myself at the time. But for the two of you...for our parents...for Amal and the baby...I had to do it. And now you're calling me a traitor! So kill me!

(**DAOUD** *grabs and hands* **NA'IM** *a butcher knife.*)

That's what I deserve, isn't it? Why don't you do it?

NA'IM. Why? Why?

DAOUD. I'm sorry...I thought it was right.

NA'IM. That makes no impression on the people you're about to meet.

DAOUD. But you...and Khalid...you understand me. Don't you? They...I'm not like you, Na'im. I'm weak. A coward, and I don't have the guts to stand up to them. That day...in the interrogation...they ruined my world. Just like that, my whole life. I can take anything. Them, the job, all this shit. What do I want? What?! A half an hour... a half an hour...on the roof of the home that I built, after I get home from work...and the sun already setting...smoke a cigarette...rest my head on Amal's stomach and laugh. That's all. But no — there's no letting up. First you get involved, and then... Nidal... and you having to run away, and now Khalid, and the leadership messing with your brains. You're a wanted man. Khalid organizes things right here in the village... and because of you, Israeli agents come to me. They knew exactly who to pick. And now I'm...it's too much already...Too much...I made a mistake...I don't know... (*Crying.*) Help me...Get me out!

NA'IM. Alright... alright ... (*Pause.*) How? How? You tell me.

DAOUD. Let's run away. Together. The three of us.

NA'IM. No good. They'll screw us all. Think of something else...

DAOUD. There's this guy who saw me when they picked me up...maybe you go to him...and tell him...that I'm in trouble...he'll come help me.

NA'IM. Who's that?

DAOUD. Issam.

KHALID. Issam? (*To* **NA'IM**) You were just over—

NA'IM. I'd kill you just not to hear that.

(**NA'IM** *launches at* **DAOUD,** *who manages to get away, as* **KHALID** *intervenes —)*

KHALID. Stop it, Na'im!

NA'IM. Issam. Issam he tells me...

KHALID. I'll get him...

NA'IM. *(Throwing* KHALID *off, and grabbing* DAOUD.*)* Issam's the biggest snitch between here and Jericho. How long have you been working with them, Daoud?

DAOUD. Two weeks...

NA'IM. Liar! If it were only two weeks...Issam wouldn't even spit at you. You wouldn't even have known he exists. No...no...it's been much longer...maybe a year...

(NA'IM *is held back by* KHALID, *but manages to push* DAOUD *over, to the floor. A wad of American fifty dollar bills falls out of* DAOUD*'s jacket as he rolls.)*

What's that? Look what falls out when they shake you. How much is there? Maybe that's the real reason, and not all your sad stories. A year, maybe a year and a half? How long? How long?!

DAOUD. A year...a year...

NA'IM. You ruined the leadership.

DAOUD. Not me...

NA'IM. You! Why are you trying to bullshit me with your stories...I was only throwing stones when you started rolling in their mud, and Khalid was still in school... and Nidal was...and Amal...Now I understand...Amal would never come from Jordan unless you promised her a house...and the money...the smelliest I know... Israeli money for the blood of my friends... in American Dollars, no less! And don't you tell me this is your salary. Or play with me again about Nidal! How could you hold that baby and call him Nidal? Didn't you gag? What will you tell the baby when he grows up and wants to know why his name is the same as that vegetable living with you? You'll make up something, and your voice won't even shake, just like it didn't tremble here...You're going to lie to him too. But deep inside, it's going to eat you up, the same way it's eating you up right now, like acid. You were the one who brought in the soldiers that shot Nidal. You knew. You invited them. You don't show a thing. You're responsible and concerned and you're a breadwinner, but underneath it's all a deep sewer. I just lifted the lid, it was enough to let the stench out. To keep up your peaceful little life, you fucked up things for everyone. You're not only a double-crosser. You're also a nothing, who could never make it on his own. You could never have a home, certainly not a wife like Amal. So you went and got all puffed up, but they'll take the wind out of you in no time, and you'll go back to being just what you are. a piece of shit that even your wife and kid — when he grows up — would rather forget. Scum...scum...

*(**NA'IM** retreats and begins to arrange his stuff to leave.)*

DAOUD. Where are they?

NA'IM. I've told you already. They're safe. I took them to mother.

DAOUD. I want my wife and my son. You hear me? You hear me, Khalid? Go, bring them here! No...I'll take care of them...no one will touch them...Na'im, you're important. I have a family now. Little Nidal. You haven't even seen him. You'll figure out a way of shutting them up, won't you, Na'im? Then you can return to the village and I'll make sure the Israelis don't touch you... we'll be together...we'll do things...no Israeli agents... no leaders...just us...we'll go out with the sheep the way we used to...and you can build homes for yourselves... get married, get horses like you wanted, and I'll have a swimming pool...remember? Without leaders...no Israeli agents...We'll throw each of them a bone...just to keep them quiet –

NA'IM. A bone...was Nidal a bone? I'm not staying here. I can't defend this thing. We're leaving, Khalid. Now. Before the leaders get here. *(Turns to leave, unlocking the door.)* Come on, Khalid. *(**KHALID** freezes.)*

DAOUD. Don't leave me alone with those animals...

NA'IM. Good bye, Daoud. Khalid!

DAOUD. *(Pulls out a pistol and aims it at* **NA'IM.***)* Not so fast, Na'im. If you budge, I'll blow your brains out. Abu Raduan betrays me, and my own brothers want to murder me. Great! Count on no one but yourself, Daoud. Just yourself. But now I'm changing everything. You leave me little choice, all of you. On your knees! On your knees! Down, I said!

*(***NA'IM*** and* **KHALID** *drop to their knees)*

Not you, Khalid. Get up.

(As **KHALID** *rises,* **DAOUD** *pulls out plastic handcuffs)*

Tie him up.

*(***KHALID*** doesn't move.)*

Tie - him - up!

*(***NA'IM*** holds out his hands and nods to* **KHALID.** **KHALID** *walks over and ties him up. He then turns to face* **DAOUD,** *and the pistol.* **DAOUD** *retreats and gathers up all the bills from the floor. He then sits down.* **KHALID** *looks at them as the lights fade out.)*

SCENE 3

(Later that night: **NA'IM** *is tied up.* **DAOUD** *is holding the pistol loosely, checking his watch every few minutes. A charged silence.)*

KHALID. Daoud.

DAOUD. Shut up, Khalid!

KHALID. Shut up?

DAOUD. Yes, and go home.

KHALID. Shut up? *(Getting worked up.)* Shut up? You too? You want me to sit here quietly and wait to see who dies first?

DAOUD. Go home, Khalid!

KHALID. Just go on, stick a bullet in his head, and you Na'im, wait for the mob to massacre him while I shut up...maybe I've got something more to learn. I'm shutting up. *(Pause.)* Why aren't you saying anything?

DAOUD. Go home, Khalid. This is not for you!

KHALID. Cleaning up Nidal's shit — is that for me? Why?

DAOUD. No Khalid...

KHALID. I've seen what you guys can do. I want a solution. From the two of you. Without blood. Daoud...the gun!

DAOUD. No way.

KHALID. The gun!

DAOUD. He'll kill me.

KHALID. Nobody's going to die. Daoud *(Gently.)* this pistol... besides from pointing it at your own brothers...it's an Israeli pistol, it's a death sentence. Final. Give me the gun.

DAOUD. My wife...and the baby?

KHALID. They're safe. *(He takes the gun from* **DAOUD.***)* No gun! Na'im? I want to untie you...*(He takes a knife and goes to cut the handcuffs, but* **NA'IM** *does not let him.)* I'm begging you. Think of a way to get us out of here. Na'im! *(***NA'IM** *is silent.)* Don't you care about him? You have your own rules. And they're always right. Save your brother's life. Na'im! *(***NA'IM** *keeps quiet.)* You promised me!

NA'IM. Go home, Khalid.

KHALID. *(Turns to* DAOUD-*)* Daoud!

DAOUD. (DAOUD *seems to be lost in thought.)* Huh?

KHALID. What do we do?

DAOUD. Ah, ...we wait.

KHALID. But, the leadership...

DAOUD. *(Amused.)* I'm not worried. What did you think? Who do you think you were dealing with? A bunch of farmers? Look, I'll show you who you're dealing with here. Abu Raduan, that son of a bitch...yeah, we worked together...But he took an insurance policy before the round-ups. He made sure I would be seen with them. Except that I have insurance too. Every time I leave the house, I make sure I tell them where I'm going, and when I'm expected back. And if I'm not in touch within a given time *(Glances at his watch.)* — which would be just about now — they come and rescue me.

KHALID. Before you came here, did you...

DAOUD. Yes. I told them. I never dreamed it would come from you...But you...the interrogation you wanted to give me...sentences...to kill me? I'm going to fuck this whole village. House by house I'll comb through it with them, pointing people out...and I know everybody. All the masked ones, they will all fall into their hands, or else they'll run away, like mice when they hear them coming. Takes them fifteen minutes to arrive. *(Pause.)* That's the solution, Khalid. You can stop worrying about me. And you'll learn not to poke your nose into things anymore.

KHALID. Daoud, you wouldn't dare bring in the...

DAOUD. I did. They're on their way. Issam is bringing them. *(To* NA'IM*)* That's right. He's a snitch. Him, you wouldn't dare go near. I arranged it with him that if I wasn't back in time...Got it now?

NA'IM. Yes. I got it. The Israeli defense forces will defend you. Great.

DAOUD. Go back to your caves in the mountains. I could

have handed you over to them. Thanks to me you're
not dead, or in jail. This year...with everything I was
doing...I was still your big brother. They didn't touch
you. Why? Ever ask yourself? "Tigers of the revolution"
...(*Laughs.*) I know exactly where you slept, what you
did, and whom you butchered.

KHALID. What are you so smug about? What are you going
to do when the army leaves?

DAOUD. Me? I'm set.

KHALID. They won't be able to protect you...

DAOUD. They'll get me out. For good. They promised...A
house, in Israel!

(NA'IM *spits at* DAOUD.)

I didn't tell them everything I know. I wanted to keep
on living here. Until you came and turned everything
upside down. Now I'm going to have to spill everything
I know...because of you! In order to get out of here. ...
Run! You don't know the trouble this village is going
to have today. Khalid, get out there before this village
turns into a madhouse. Run home, get Amal ready...
and the family. We're leaving the village.

KHALID. And Nidal?

DAOUD. Him too.

KHALID. And me?

DAOUD. You'll come with me. To a place they'll give us. A
house. Some land. A job. Eh? Far away from all this
shit. We'll live like human beings.

KHALID. And Na'im?

DAOUD. Let him go back to the mountains.

KHALID. And the people in the village...the ones who...you're
going to turn them in?

DAOUD. Forget them, Khalid. Think about yourself, about
your future. Life is too short for big wars. You don't
have to love the Israelis. But we've got to go on living.
And here...we have no life anymore.

KHALID. Thanks to you!

DAOUD. Bullshit! Things were never good here. They never
will be. What do you say? Decide! We don't have all
night. The army will be here soon.

KHALID. I won't go as far as the door with you. Just thinking
of what you've offered us makes me sick. You used me.
All those questions you always asked...about the rally...
(To NA'IM*)* I told him about it...I didn't think...and ...
poor Nidal...because of me...The army's coming here?
That's how you'll solve your problem? How can I walk
around the village, after you...why? Why? Why?

DAOUD. To stay alive. Just think what Na'im's people would
have done to me if I hadn't. You know what they do?
They chop off your prick and skin you, and you're still
alive. That's what they mean by courage. And don't let
them tell you otherwise. They're scared of the Israelis,
so they let out their venom, right here, on us. They're
heroes...against whom? Against ordinary people, so sti-
fled by the Israelis that they don't have any strength
anymore. They're told how to behave, what to believe,
what to think, when to eat, and when to shit! And if they
don't like you, they kill you. Without a sentence. Just
like that. Because a couple of kids think they should.
(To NA'IM*)* And you're telling me the Israeli military
trials are a joke? And who are you? Who appointed
you? Tell me one good thing you did for our people!
One! Just don't give me your fancy phrases because I
don't understand them. All I know is how much blood,
how much of our blood you've spilled for them. You
and your militias killed more Palestinians then the
Israelis!—

KHALID. You didn't answer me. You could have been passive. Why squeal? Why?

NA'IM. What do you want from him? He has nothing to
say. Every word he utters only buries him deeper. Just
look, see what he tied me up with? *(Waving his plastic
handcuffs.)* You know what these are, Khalid? Plastic
handcuffs, from the Israeli army...*(Pause.)* You know,
Khalid, when the Israelis first came to our village, I was

seven...Ataf and me, we took a few other kids and organized an army...kids. Daoud didn't want to take part. He sat on a hill with the soldiers. They gave him candy, he sang and danced for them. I was so ashamed. Me... since I was a kid, I never stopped dreaming the occupation would end. *(To* **DAOUD**.*)* And you...my brother... what do you dream of? A house? In Israel? You're finished. There's nothing for you. I heard your offer to Khalid...They'll stick you with hookers and junkies, on the smelliest street in the lousiest slum. Fifty years you'll be licking their asses, but you'll still be an Arab snitch who sold his people for money. Even Arabs in Israel will spit at you. Is that how your son will grow up? *(Shows his tied-up hands.)* Like this? In disgrace? You don't have to fight. If only you took it seriously...a little...in your heart...but no, it's all words for you. You can't turn it into money, it doesn't mean anything to you. Look at me. Me...I fight. Hard. And brutal, because I think we could make it. Nobody's giving away anything for free. It's a struggle! Otherwise we don't deserve what we get. What you call 'fancy phrases'...You, no matter how you try to turn it around, you sold yourself to be a slave. Nothing more. I'm not telling you all this just to preach. (**NA'IM**, *still handcuffed, embraces* **DAOUD**) You're my big brother. I'm leaving you now. You're going to climb to the top of the mosque and shout into the loudspeakers for the whole village to hear. "I'm Daoud. I handed over your sons, I blew up your homes. I'm a squealer, this is my punishment." And then you'll jump. You'll jump. It'll be fast and painless, and more important, it's the only way you'll save your name. And ours. The only way. Don't let anyone touch you, because if they do, you'll not only die like a dog, but your son will be cursed as well. Get up, my brother. Get up and do it.

(Pause. **DAOUD** *almost manages to raise, but eventually remains sitting and turns away, checking the time.* **NA'IM** *weeps)*

I'm sorry, Khalid...you know how badly I wanted...

KHALID. *(Cutting off* **NA'IM***'s handcuffs)* Get out of here, Na'im. The army will be here any minute. (**NA'IM** *shakes his head.)*

DAOUD. Khalid?

KHALID. What else do you want?

DAOUD. You've got to help me. Just once more, or I'm dead.

NA'IM. What happened to the army? Did they forget you?

DAOUD. *(Ignoring* **NA'IM***.)* It's my life. You said so yourself.

NA'IM. You did call the army, didn't you?

DAOUD. Yes...but...something went wrong. They should have been here long ago...

KHALID. What can I do? *(To himself.)* What can I do?

DAOUD. I want you to go to Issam and tell him...tell him what's going on...that the arrangement we made...no... there's no time. Tell him to go outside right now, and shoot in the air, and shout that the army is on its way. That'll scare them off. I don't get it...he was — for sure — he was going to tell them...

NA'IM. If he were alive.

DAOUD. What? Liar!

NA'IM. Why aren't they coming then?

DAOUD. No one can touch him...

NA'IM. The way he looks now, no one would want to touch him...

DAOUD. No way...it's not true!

NA'IM. Before coming here...(**NA'IM** *produces a bloodstained shirt.)*

DAOUD. I talked to him just before I came here...

NA'IM. You were the last one...before I "talked" to him...

(**NA'IM** *tosses the blood soaked shirt towards* **DAOUD**.*)*

DAOUD. But he has a gun...

(**NA'IM** *pulls out a pistol just like* **DAOUD***'s)*

NA'IM. This?

(**DAOUD** *is silent.* **NA'IM** *places the gun on a cinder block.)*

KHALID. *(Terrified.)* What do we do now?

DAOUD. *(Sobered.)* I am going to die. His friends will slaughter me.

KHALID. Daoud, get out. Run away on foot...you have a gun.

DAOUD. It won't help. They're waiting for me at the door. In every corner. No, I'm staying here. Let them kill me before your eyes, right here, in this place you brought me to. You'll watch, then you'll have to go on living. I betrayed you, and now I'm going to sit here and wait for my punishment. Only you can save me, and I'm telling you that if you do that. you'll be saving yourselves as well. I'm finished. You decide.

KHALID. *(To* NA'IM*)* Go outside and talk to them.

NA'IM. There's no chance.

KHALID. No mater what he's done, he doesn't deserve to die like this.

NA'IM. He's got a gun. He can do it quick.

KHALID. Na'im...

NA'IM. *(On the verge of tears.)* I can't...I can't...

(Pause.)

KHALID. Come on, Daoud. I'll get you out of the village. *(They rush to the door, but it is locked.)* Give me the key, Na'im.

*(*NA'IM *is passive.* KHALID *pulls out the key from his hands. They turn to leave. Loud knocks on the door; they grow increasingly louder. The two freeze, then step back. Looks are exchanged. Eventually,* KHALID *stabs* DAOUD *to death with a butcher knife while embracing him.* DAOUD *collapses into* NA'IM*'s arms. The knocks resume.)*

NA'IM. Open the door, Khalid.

(Lights fade to black.)

THE END

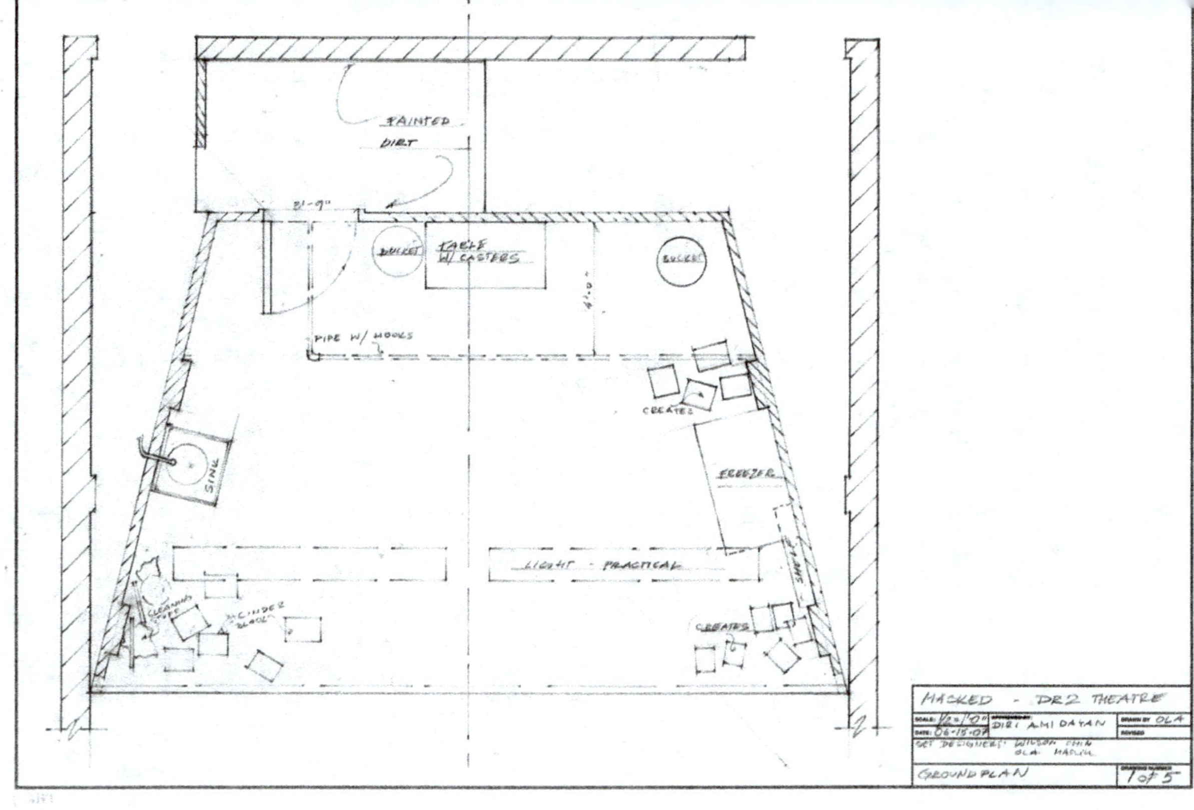

PAINTED
DIRT
8'-9"
BUCKET
TABLE W/ CASTERS
BUCKET
4'-0"
PIPE W/ HOOKS
CRATES
FREEZER
SINK
CLEANING TUBE
CINDER BLOCK
LIGHT - PRACTICAL
CRATES
SHELF
MASKED - DR2 THEATRE
SCALE: 1/2"=1'0"
DATE: 06-15-07
DIR: AMI DAYAN
DRAWN BY: OLA
APPROVED BY:
REVISED:
SET DESIGNERS: WILSON CHIN
OLA MASLIK
GROUND PLAN
DRAWING NUMBER
1 of 5

OTHER TITLES AVAILABLE FROM SAMUEL FRENCH

FEMININE ENDING
Sarah Treem

Full Length / Dark Comedy / 3m, 2f / Various, Unit set
Amanda, twenty-five, wants to be a great composer. But at the moment, she's living in New York City and writing advertising jingles to pay the rent while her fiancée, Jack pursues his singing career. So when Amanda's mother, Kim, calls one evening from New Hampshire and asks for her help with something she can't discuss over the phone, Amanda is only too happy to leave New York. Once home, Kim reveals that she's leaving Amanda father and needs help packing. Amanda balks and ends up (gently) hitting the postman, who happens to be her first boyfriend. They spend the night together in an apple orchard, where Amanda tries to tell Billy how her life got sidetracked. It has something to do with being a young woman in a profession that only recognizes famous men. Billy acts like he might have the answer, but doesn't. Neither does Amanda's mother. Or, for that matter, her father. A Feminine Ending is a gentle, bittersweet comedy about a girl who knows what she wants but not quite how to get it. Her parents are getting divorced, her fiancée is almost famous, her first love reappears, and there's a lot of noise in her head but none of it is music. Until the end.

"Darkly comic. *Feminine Ending* has undeniable wit."
- New York Post

"Appealingly outlandish humor."
- The New York Times

"Courageous. The 90-minute piece swerves with nerve and naivete. Sarah Treem has a voice all her own."
- Newsday

OTHER TITLES AVAILABLE FROM SAMUEL FRENCH

MAURITIUS
Theresa Rebeck

Comedy / 3m, 2f / Interior

Stamp collecting is far more risky than you think. After their mother's death, two estranged half-sisters discover a book of rare stamps that may include the crown jewel for collectors. One sister tries to collect on the windfall, while the other resists for sentimental reasons. In this gripping tale, a seemingly simple sale becomes dangerous when three seedy, high-stakes collectors enter the sisters' world, willing to do anything to claim the rare find as their own.

"(Theresa Rebeck's) belated Broadway bow, the only original play by a woman to have its debut on Broadway this fall."
- Robert Simonson, *The New York Times*

"*Mauritius* caters efficiently to a hunger that Broadway hasn't been gratifying in recent years. That's the corkscrew-twist drama of suspense… she has strewn her script with a multitude of mysteries."
- Ben Brantley, *The New York Times*

"Theresa Rebeck is a slick playwright… Her scenes have a crisp shape, her dialogue pops, her characters swagger through an array of showy emotion, and she knows how to give a plot a cunning twist."
-John Lahr, *The New Yorker*